Presented to

_____

from

_____

_____

Date _____

Bedtime Stories

PRECIOUS™ MOMENTS

Bedtime Stories

Text by

Samuel J.
and
Jon David Butcher

Debbie Ann
and
Steven Craig Wiersma

Illustrations by

Samuel J. Butcher

BAKER BOOK HOUSE
Grand Rapids, Michigan 49516

First printing, January 1989
Second printing, March 1989
Third printing, June 1989
Fourth printing, August 1989
Fifth printing, September 1989
Sixth printing, October 1989
Seventh printing, January 1990
Eighth printing, February 1990
Ninth printing, June 1990

Betty De Vries
Editor and Production Coordinator

Library of Congress Cataloging-in-Publication Data

Precious moments bedtime stories.

   Summary: presents twenty-two stories dealing with
such themes as bedtime, school, family, friendship, and
animals.
   1. Children's stories, American. [1. Short stories]
I. Butcher, Samuel J. (Samuel John), 1939–
II. Title: Bedtime stories.
PZ5.P784 1988   [E]   88-24047
ISBN 0-8010-0959-6

Printed in the United States of America

Contents

3. Animal Tales

4. School Days

5. Sleepytime Stories

Preface

Bedtime—that precious time when parent and child have their own little world for a few minutes. It's a time for sharing, reflecting, confiding, and cuddling.

These bedtime stories help to set the tone for the quiet time. They will help children learn about themselves, their world, and the people in it. A child will be encouraged to talk to God just before he or she drifts off to sleep.

Sam Butcher and his children have written these delightful stories. Sam's charming *Precious Moments* drawings give life and interest to the stories. Children are attracted to the expressive eyes and the soft colors which easily convey happiness or sadness—and often there is an unforgettable touch of humor. The result is a favorite storybook, a treasure that will be read and re-read.

So, settle yourself in a comfortable chair, gather your child in your arms, pick out a special story, and get set to enjoy some very precious moments.

The Publisher

1 Friends
and Play

A Special Birthday

Laura had saved a very special present to open last. It was a birthday present from Grandma and Grandpa. They almost always got her a doll, but she had no idea what was in this tiny box. She sat down with her two favorite dolls and opened her last present.

It was a beautiful music box! Laura

lifted the top and laughed when she heard the little song.

"What is this?" she asked her dolls. They just smiled back at her as she took a little card out of the box.

Two ten-dollar bills fell out! There was also a little note that said:

> Dear Laura,
> We wanted to buy you a doll, but we didn't know which one you would like. So this birthday we want you to get a very special doll, one that you can keep for your own little girl.
>
> Love, Grandma
> and Grandpa

Laura was excited. She knew just which doll she wanted. There was one little girl doll at the toy store that she liked so very much. She looked at the

money again and said, "Mom, with this money I can buy *two* dolls—one for me and one for my best friend Becky."

"Maybe you should think about that a little more, Laura. Grandma and Grandpa want you to have a very special doll. Maybe you'll find one."

"But, Mom, if I buy two of them, both Becky and I will have a special doll. She would like to have a new doll too. The only one she has is one her sister played with."

"Hi! Laura!" called Becky. "May I see your presents?"

Becky and Laura looked at the music box and the other nice gifts.

"Becky, I'm so excited! With my birthday money I can buy *two* dolls, one for you and one for me. Just think of the fun we're going to have."

"Well, Laura, I think you should get just one doll, the prettiest one you can find. That's your birthday money and you

should use it for yourself," said Becky. "We can take turns playing with her. I know you have a favorite doll picked out at the toy store."

"C'mon!" said Laura. "Let's go to the store now."

The best friends skipped along, happy

to be together. They looked in the window of the toy store and saw so many wonderful toys—stuffed animals, blocks, even a Jack-in-the-box. In one corner of the window was a beautiful baby doll just waiting for a new mother.

"Isn't she pretty?" gasped Laura. "She must have just come in."

"She's adorable!!" agreed Becky. "Let's go in and see if we can hold her."

Laura picked up the doll and cuddled her. "Mm-m-m! I'd like to take you home! I'll call you Baby Sue."

Laura and Becky took turns carrying Baby Sue around as the two friends looked at all the other dolls in the store. Both agreed that none of the other dolls was as pretty as little Baby Sue.

"It looks like Baby Sue is the one for you," said Becky, who was just a little sad that Laura had enough money for only *one* Baby Sue.

Laura smiled at the doll. "I'm going to put you back in your corner, Baby Sue. But, maybe I'll come back for you."

"Why didn't you buy Baby Sue, Laura?" asked Becky.

"I want to talk to my mom first," said Laura, with a twinkle in her eye. "C'mon, I'll race you home."

That night Laura and her Mother talked a long time about Baby Sue and Becky.

"Mom, Becky is too proud to say she'd like a Baby Sue of her own. But I saw the look in her eye as she held her. Becky has only one worn-out doll. I just wouldn't be happy playing with Baby Sue, even if I shared her with Becky, because I know Becky would love to have a doll of her own. I wish I could give Becky a Baby Sue. . . but I want a Baby Sue, too."

"Hmmm," said Mother. "Maybe there is a way to solve this problem. I want to

think about it tonight. Let's pray about it. Now you go to sleep. Sweet dreams!"

Laura could see that Mother had a special surprise sparkle in her eyes the next morning but Mother wouldn't tell her the happy secret.

"Let's check the toy store today," said Laura when Becky came over to play that afternoon.

Together the friends skipped to the store. They looked for Baby Sue's corner in the window and. . . SHE WASN'T THERE!!!

"Maybe they moved her," said Becky. "We could look inside."

Whoosh! They opened the door and ran to the doll section. No Baby Sue!

"She's gone! I wonder if someone bought her! What will we do now?" cried Laura.

Slowly the two friends walked back to Laura's house. They had very sad faces

and once in a while a tear came down a cheek.

Becky snuffed back a sob.

Laura snuffed back two sobs.

They were VERY sad! Mother was waiting for the two friends. She was wearing her special surprise smile and even her eyes were sparkling.

"Come in, girls! There's a surprise in the den," she said, with that special smile.

"Nothing, NOTHING!!! Not even a surprise could make us happy today, Mom," cried Laura.

"Oh, why?" asked Mother.

"Baby Sue is gone! She's not at the toy store," Becky sobbed.

"Really?" said Mother, who didn't sound at all surprised to hear that news.

There were two packages in the corner of the den. They were exactly alike, except one said, "TO BECKY." The other one said, "TO LAURA."

"Okay," said Mother. "Unwrap them together.

O-N-E, T-W-O, THREE, GO!"

Rustle, rustle, rustle! Then no sound at all, not even a breathing sound. Laura lifted a baby doll out of her box. Becky lifted a baby doll out of *her* box.

"Baby Sue!" said Laura.

"Oh, look at this," cried Becky, "I have a Baby Sue, too."

Both of the girls giggled with delight.

"I know, Becky, let's call yours Baby Lu and call mine Baby Sue," Laura said with a big smile.

Now it was Mother's turn to wipe a tear off her cheek. But it was a happy tear.

The Echo

Johnny was lonesome, VERY LONE-SOME!!! He and his mother and father had just moved to the country. There were some dandy hills and some exciting caves in the hills near the river. It was almost a perfectly nice place to live. But Johnny had no one to play with. NO ONE!!! This made Johnny sad, super sad. Today he

was mighty sad and very lonesome. It just wasn't a good day for Johnny.

He climbed to the top of the hill to see if

there was anyone around to play with. No, Johnny couldn't see any boys. He couldn't see any girls. He couldn't see any dogs. He couldn't see any kittens. He was alone on the hill. He couldn't find anyone!

"I wonder if there is another boy on the top of that hill over there. It's too far away to see anybody. Maybe if I yell, somebody will hear me," Johnny said to himself.

Johnny took a deep breath and yelled as loud as he could, "H-E-L-L-O!"

To his surprise, he heard, "H-e-l-l-o!" from across the valley.

"Well, what do you know about that?" Johnny chuckled. "There is a little boy over there on the top of that hill and he sounds like he's about my age."

"How are you?" Johnny called.

"How are you?" came back from across the valley.

"I'm fine," Johnny answered. "How are you?"

"I'm fine. How are you?"

"I already said I'm fine," Johnny screamed.

"I already said I'm fine," came back from across the valley.

"Hmm-mm," Johnny said softly, almost to himself, "I wonder what kind of a boy is over there. Every time I call to him, he says the very same thing back to me. Is he trying to play some kind of game with me?"

"Hey, are you trying to be funny?" Johnny snapped.

"Hey, are you trying to be funny?" came back from across the valley.

"OK, wise guy, I'm coming over to fix you good!" Johnny bellowed.

"OK, wise guy, I'm coming over to fix you good!" was the reply.

Johnny's face got red. He was angry. He thought of some not-so-nice things to say to that "kid" on the next hill. "Oh, oh,

what if he's bigger than I am? What if he's a great big guy? What if he's ten feet tall?"

Johnny was SCARED. He was really

scared. Suddenly he ran down the hill, stormed into the house, and scrambled under the blanket on his bed.

"Why, Johnny!" said Mother. "What on earth is wrong?"

"It's that kid on the other hill, Mom. I was trying to be friendly to him when all of a sudden he started saying bad things to me."

"Hmm-m that's strange. Are you sure you didn't start saying bad things to him first?" Mother asked.

"No, Mom, I'm really sure. He started it," said Johnny, just peeking out from under the blanket.

"Well, I have an idea," Mother said. "Let's go to the hill again and I'll listen while you tell that boy you are sorry that you said mean things to him."

"I can't do that, Mom," Johnny cried. "You don't understand. He's bigger than I am and he will never make up with me."

"C'mon, I'll go with you," said Mother.
"Let's go now. We'll just give it a try."

Slowly Johnny crawled out from under
his blanket. He didn't want to climb that
hill and talk to that big mean kid again.

He'd had enough hassle from him for one day. In fact, he didn't want to talk to that kid for a long time—maybe never. Johnny would rather be sad and lonesome than to talk to that meanie. But Johnny knew he had to obey his mother. So off they went.

Johnny's knees knocked as he slowly walked to the top of the hill. Mother was walking with him but that didn't help one bit—well, maybe only a little bit. When they reached the top, Johnny looked over the valley and then slowly looked at the great big hill on the other side. He stared at the bottom of the hill and then slowly looked up the hill to the very top.

"I sure hope that he's not mad anymore," Johnny whispered to himself. "Anyway, now that I'm up here I may as well do what Mother said."

"I'm very sorry," Johnny said, not nearly as loud as the first time he talked to the "big mean kid."

"I'm very sorry," the voice replied.

"I can't believe it, Mom," Johnny said. "He's sorry too."

"Do you want to be my friend?" Johnny asked.

"Do you want to be my friend?" the voice replied.

"Yes, I want to be your friend," Johnny shouted.

"Yes, I want to be your friend," the voice shouted back.

Mom and Johnny hugged each other as Johnny said, "Mom! Now I've found a new friend. That kid over there isn't angry with me anymore."

Mother just smiled at Johnny.

"You see," she said, "being nice to someone is the best way to make a friend."

Mother didn't tell Johnny the secret about the echo. They were going to talk about that when she tucked him in at bedtime.

Yen Finds a Friend

"Grandfather is here," Yen's mother said, peeking into the kitchen where Yen was eating his breakfast.

Yen had just moved to America from halfway across the world. All of his friends were in China, far, far away, and Yen was very LONELY. But today was a very special day. Grandfather was going

41

to take him to the zoo. Yen had never been to a zoo and he was very excited.

"Hello, Grandfather," the little boy said. Grandfather gave Yen a big hug.

"I've missed you, Yen. I have a present for you on this special day," said Grandfather.

Yen tore off the paper. Inside was a bright red T-shirt. The white letters on the front and back said USA.

"Oh, thank you, Grandfather," the little boy said. "I'm going to wear it today. I'll be back in just a minute after I change shirts."

When Yen and Grandfather got to the zoo, the first thing they saw was a big animal with strange skin. It looked like the skin that shoes are made of.

"He's so big, Grandfather," said Yen. "What is his name? The words on the sign look almost as big as he is."

"That's a rhinoceros!" said Grandfa-

ther. "You will see many more strange animals here. Look over there. Do you know what that one is called?"

Yen shook his head. "Well, she has a big pocket in front. Is she called some kind of pocket?"

"No," said Grandfather. "She is a kangaroo. The pouch in front is where she carries her baby. A kangaroo baby is called a joey. Kangaroos come from Australia. That's even farther away than China."

"I wonder if she's lonely. She left all her friends in Australia," said Yen sadly.

Yen's grandfather smiled and gave Yen a big hug. "She doesn't look lonely to me. I think I see a smile on her face. She's made many new friends here.

"See that blue bird? He's singing a song just for her. And there

is another kangaroo. Over there are some
bunnies just waiting to play with her. I
think she likes her new home."

They walked down a path and came to
a sign that said, GIRAFFE BARN. There
were tall trees and long grass.

Yen pointed to an animal with a very,

very long neck. "Where did this animal live, Grandfather?"

"Let's see, I think he came from Africa," said Grandfather. "He probably lived close to the elephants that we just passed. Maybe they were neighbors in Africa and that's why the zoo keeper made them neighbors here. Doesn't that giraffe look happy? I think he likes his home."

"Getting hungry, Yen?" asked Grandfather. "Are you ready for a snack?"

"Yes, I am, Grandfather," said Yen. "That sign says POPCORN. Let's try some of it!"

"Good choice," said Grandfather, as he bought some popcorn.

Yen and Grandfather sat on a bench to rest because Grandfather wanted to talk with Yen. "Sometimes," Grandfather said, "you can feel very lonely in a new place. But now that we've seen how happy the animals are in their new home with

their new friends, maybe you can under-stand that you can be happy in a new place, too.

"You know," Grandfather said, "one day I read a story in the Bible about some very lonely men. They were friends of Jesus and they thought Jesus was going to go away and leave them. Jesus knew how lonely they felt. You see, once he was so lonely, too. He didn't have any friends. Every friend had left him because they were afraid.

"Jesus knew that there was only one way to cheer up his friends. He made a special promise: 'I will never leave you. I will always be with you.'

"Yen, Jesus has promised me this, too. And he will give you the same promise if you believe him. He will always be your BEST FRIEND. And I believe he will also soon give you some special friends. Let's talk to Jesus by praying to him now. We'll

ask him to be your special friend and to give you new friends and help you to be happy in your new home."

Yen felt much better after their little talk.

"Now, I know that sometimes you will miss some things you had in your old home. That's why I want you to meet a very special animal. C'mon, I'll introduce you."

Now Yen was excited. Who could Grandfather be talking about? Who would want to be Yen's special animal? They walked all the way to the other side of the zoo. Finally they stopped at a large bamboo grove. And rolling on the ground was. . .

"A PANDA!" Yen shouted. "Oh, Grandfather, he came all the way from China, just like me!"

The fuzzy little black and white panda looked up at Yen and seemed to smile.

Then he got up and walked over close to where Yen was watching.

"Smile, Yen, please," said a big man who seemed to come from nowhere. "I want to take a picture of the two of you. In fact, I'll take two pictures, one for me and one for you. I have a special kind of camera and you can have your very own picture in just a minute."

So Yen smiled, a

VERY BIG SMILE. And the panda walked even closer to Yen.

Snap! Snap!

"Here's your picture," said the man. "It's a good one. Both of you seem to like each other."

"Thanks, Sir," said Yen. "Thank you so much."

Yen put the picture on the bulletin board in his bedroom. Soon that special picture was surrounded by pictures of smiling boys and girls—Yen's new friends. You see, he did make new friends just as Grandfather had promised.

Little Beaver

Little Beaver, a little Indian boy, lived many, many years ago. He was sad because he had no one to play with. He was the youngest boy in the tribe. All the other boys were older, old enough to be Indian braves. And Indian braves were much too busy to play with a little boy.

"I'll never be old enough to be a brave," Little Beaver said to his mother.

"You just wait," she said. "I'm sure when you grow up you will be the best Indian brave there ever was."

Mother was usually right, and Little Beaver smiled whenever he thought about her promise that he would be the best Indian brave ever.

One day Little Beaver was so lonely that he decided to find a friend no matter how long it took. He climbed to the top of the highest hill and made a

Little Beaver

little fire. When there was lots of smoke, he took his blanket and covered the fire. By letting out little bits of smoke at a time, he sent a smoke signal, a message to any Indian who could read smoke signals.

Little Beaver's message said: "My name is Little Beaver. I am sad. Will you come and play with me?"

There were no answering smoke signals from the other hills. Little Beaver sat down to wait, just to make sure.

Rustle, rustle, RUSTLE! Something was in the bushes. Something was coming toward Little Beaver. Was it somebody to play with? Little Beaver quietly walked over to the bush.

Then he saw the noisemaker— a lovely Indian princess carrying a baby doll papoose on her back.

"Hello!" she smiled. "My name is Morningstar."

"Hello!" said Little Beaver.

57

"I saw your smoke signal and I came here right away," Morningstar said happily.

"Oh, I'm really glad you did," said Little Beaver, "because I'm so lonely and I truly need a friend."

Little Beaver

The little princess smiled. "You look so strong and brave. Can you shoot an arrow straight for a long way?"

"Oh, yes, I am brave, very brave," said Little Beaver proudly. "And just watch me—I can shoot an arrow just like a grown-up. See that bunny over there?"

Little Beaver quickly pulled a little string on his bow and an arrow flew into the air.

"OUCH!!!" cried the bunny, as he rubbed his backside where the arrow hit him.

Little Beaver felt so bad that tears fell down his cheeks. "Oh, I am so sorry, Bunny. I wanted to show Morningstar how far I could shoot an arrow. I didn't mean to hurt you."

The bunny looked up and smiled at Little Beaver. Then it hopped away.

"Oh, dear! I know the princess saw me cry. I guess I really am not very brave. I'll

have to make her believe that I didn't mean to hurt the bunny." Little Beaver was sure the princess wouldn't want him for a friend now.

"Little Beaver," a gentle voice called. It was Princess Morningstar. "You are good with your bow and arrow, but even more than that, you are very, very kind. A missionary came to our village and taught us that kindness is the most important gift of all. Then my father told me to look for a friend who is kind."

Little Beaver could hardly believe his ears. Morningstar still wanted to be his friend.

"Please, Little Beaver, let's go to see my father. When I tell him about your kindness he will be happy to hear about my special friend."

Quickly Little Beaver and Morningstar got into his canoe and paddled to her village. Little Beaver met her father, a

tall, tall Indian. Morningstar told the story of Little Beaver and the bunny.

The chief smiled. "Little Beaver, the Bible says, 'Be kind to one another.' I want Morningstar to have friends who are kind to each other and to all the creatures God has made. I hope you and Morningstar have many happy days playing together. And when you get older and bigger I'm sure that you will be a kind and great Indian brave, perhaps the best one ever."

2 Family Times

I Can Do It!

"What do you think, Grandpa!" asked Timmy. "Will we catch lots of fish today?"

The pond was sparkling as it caught the bright sun's rays. The birds were singing, happy to be out on such a sunny day.

"Sure, Timmy," said Grandpa. "Some days are just made for fishing. . . and this is one of them."

Splash! a fish had jumped. Then another. . . and another. There really were big ones in the pond.

Timmy was a new fisherman and Grandpa showed him how to tie on a hook and then a small sinker. Next Timmy slipped a red-and-white bobber on his line so he could tell when a fish nibbled at the worm. Putting a wiggly, slippery worm on the hook was hard and Grandpa made Timmy try again and again until he had it on just right.

"OK, fish! Now I'm ready!" said Timmy. He waited for a big whopper to bite. But nothing happened.

"Hey," said Grandpa, "I've got one!" And he did, a beautiful bluegill. He soon caught a sunfish, then another bluegill.

Timmy began to feel sad because he hadn't caught any fish and Grandpa already had three. Suddenly the red-and-white bobber took a nose dive. Timmy had

a fish on his line. He jerked the pole and began to bring the fish to shore. He just knew this was a B-I-G one! Timmy's eyes lit up and his muscles bulged.

Snap!! the fish spit out the hook. Splash!!! the fish fell back into the pond.

There was nothing left but a limp line, a shiny hook, and a very sad Timmy.

"Grandpa, I lost him! I'm no good at anything." Timmy tried hard not to cry.

"Aw, Timmy, I'm sorry your fish got away. I lose a lot of fish, too. It happens all the time. Try again."

Timmy baited the hook and threw out
the line. TUG! Sure enough, there was a

fish on his line. Timmy became so excited that he waved his arms and spun around a couple of times. He just wasn't very good at pulling fish in. Timmy became all tangled up in the line and the little fish landed on top of Timmy's head. The fish was much too small to keep.

"Grandpa, I'm just NO GOOD AT ANYTHING!!!" Timmy sighed loudly.

Grandpa put his arm around Timmy's shoulders.

"Timmy, do you know that everyone is good at something? All you have to do is find out what you're good at and then have fun working at it."

"Really, Grandpa? What do you think I would be good at?"

"Well, I'm not sure. When King David of Israel was a little boy, he loved to shoot a sling. He practiced with his sling every day. When he became older, he used a sling to kill a mighty giant. But as great

71

a warrior as David was, he could also play the harp better than anyone else in his whole kingdom."

"Well, I'm not good with a slingshot, either," Timmy confessed. "But I can play the guitar a little bit."

"So there you are," said Grandpa, as he gave Timmy a hug. "And I know you can play even better. All it takes is time and practice."

"Whoops! There goes my bobber again! This time, you little whale, I'm going to get you." He pulled in the line quickly. . . and carefully.

There wasn't a little whale wiggling on the hook but it was a bluegill, a big bluegill, even bigger than the bluegills Grandpa had caught.

"You're right, Grandpa! I can do it if I try! I just love to fish!"

Plop! there went the red-and-white bobber on the water again.

"Oh, look, Timmy, it looks like you have another one," Grandpa said.

Timmy laughed, "Yes, I do, Grandpa. I'm learning how to be a fisherman. Someday maybe I'll be as good as you are."

Grandpa chuckled, "You probably will, Timmy. But I hope you'll be even better than I am at playing the guitar. C'mon, it's time to go home and cook these fish. And maybe you'd like to do some practicing this afternoon."

"Sure, Grandpa," said Timmy. "Just wait! Soon I'll play a special song just for you."

74

The Rainy Day

"Oh, no! *Not rain again!*" Billy grumbled. "I want the rain to stop NOW!"

Billy was in a not-so-very-good mood this morning. His mother called it Billy's BAD mood. It was almost Billy's VERY BAD mood.

"Well, why don't you do something fun?"

"Don't want to do anything fun. I want to go outside and swing and run and play ball."

"Read a book," said Mother.

"Don't want to read a book," said Billy.

"Watch TV," said Mother.

"Don't want to watch TV," said Billy.

Billy's BAD mood was getting worse. The corners of his mouth were turning down and down and down.

Mother put her arm around Billy and used her it's-time-to-behave voice.

"So, now you get to help me. Go upstairs this very minute, get dressed, and then clean out your messy, messy closet."

"Aw, Mom, do I have to?" Billy moaned.

"Yes, you do. And go upstairs NOW!"

Billy stomped up the steps. He didn't like rainy days at all. He liked cleaning out his closet even less.

He opened the closet door. His closet was a mess—a messy, messy mess.

Bang! he picked up a shoe and threw it out. Bang! the next shoe just missed his dog.

"Phew, these socks smell so bad. So do these old tennis shoes." Out they went with two softer bangs.

In a corner was a dusty old book.

"What's this book all about? I don't remember seeing it. It even smells dusty."

Billy opened the book to the first page.

There was some writing on the inside cover.

To our precious son
BILLY
From Mother and Father
1908

"1908? I wasn't even born until a few years ago," mumbled Billy. "Oh, now I get it. This book was given to my great grandpa Bill when he was just a little boy."

Billy carefully turned to another page. It said, "A Bible Story Book for Children."

Suddenly a wonderful world of adventure opened up for Billy—stories about kings and a giant and a chariot of fire. Then he read about a donkey who talked, a man who walked on water, and a great big net full of fish.

Billy kept turning page after page. He smiled when he read the story of the Good

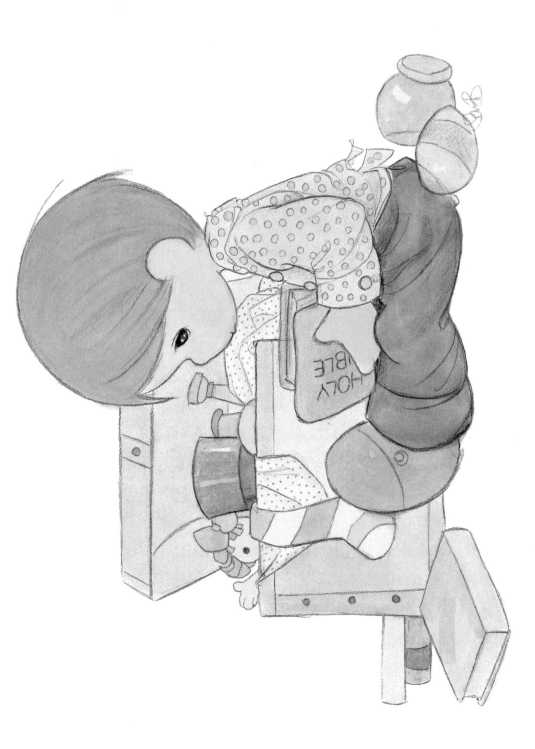

Shepherd. Billy imagined that he was also hunting for a lost sheep and how happy he was when he finally found that sheep.

Billy wished he could have been one of the children who climbed on Jesus' lap.

Then he imagined he was on a missionary journey with the apostle Paul. It felt so good to tell people the good news about Jesus.

After the two loud BANGS and two softer bangs, Billy's mother didn't hear any noises—either soft ones or loud ones. Mother tiptoed upstairs and peeked into Billy's room. There he was, half in and half out of his closet, reading and reading and reading.

"Billy, you've been up here almost two hours. Look! the sun is shining. Now you can go outside."

"Mom, I've found the best book in my closet. It's about kings and a giant and it

tells about when Jesus lived on earth, and. . . ."

"I'm glad you found something to do, Billy. And that is a very special book. Your great-grandfather read that one when he was just a boy."

Billy was in a good mood now. He was happy. The corners of his mouth curled up in a big smile.

The sun was out.

He was going to run and swing and play ball in the park.

His friends were calling him.

And he had found a special treasure while it was raining.

Philip Learns a Lesson

Philip and his dog Tippy left home as soon as it was light. They were off to the river to catch some big fish. But Philip was still sleepy and the bright, warm sun made Philip feel very cozy. He closed his eyes. Soon he was almost sleeping.

Tug, tug, TUG! Something was tugging at the fishing line. This wasn't just a little

nibble. This fish wanted the worm and line and pole. Was it a ten-pounder?

Philip opened his eyes and shook his head. There was his bobber on top of the water. No fish! Not even a little one.

Tug, tug, TUG! TUG!

"Tippy, what are you doing?" Tippy was tugging on the line. He wanted to play.

"Oh, all right," Philip said, as he took a ball out of his fishing bag. "Let's play. I'm never going to catch anything with this crummy pole anyway. When Dad comes home tonight I'm going to tell him that I need a real fishing pole, not just a tree branch."

As soon as Dad settled down in his favorite chair, Philip plunked on the floor in front of him and said very quietly, "Dad, I have something important to talk about."

"What is it, Philip?"

Philip looked sad. "I've been using the

same crummy old branch for fishing all summer, and I never catch anything with it. I need a real pole, Dad. None of the other kids has to use a stick. Amy caught three fish yesterday with her new pole. And do you know what? Her dad bought it for her."

Father smiled as he said, "Philip, you

can have a new fishing pole any time. But you will have to buy it yourself."

"But, Dad," Philip protested, "I don't have any money!"

"I could buy that pole for you, Philip, but I'll tell you why I'm not going to. Remember that sled you just had to have last winter? You used it twice and then decided that sliding in a cardboard box was better. I think if you earn the money to buy the fishing pole yourself, you will appreciate it much more."

That night Philip made some plans. He drifted off to sleep thinking about mowing lawns and raking and weeding gardens.

After breakfast, Philip ran down to Mrs. Bronner's house to see if he could walk her dog. Mrs. Bronner was happy to see Philip and offered to pay him for exercising her dog. This was fun. Even Tippy liked the company as the three of them took a long walk and run in the woods.

Clink! there went some coins in Philip's piggy bank. But Philip needed more money, so off he went to ask the neighbors if they needed help with weeding or mowing. He was busy all morning and he had some more money to put in the bank. Clink! Clink! Poof. He even had a dollar bill to put in.

The next day was hot, too hot to work hard. "Tippy, even you are hot! I know, I'll sell some lemonade. This is just the right day for a cold drink." So, with a few hard bangs with his dad's hammer, Philip made a lemonade stand. Next, he fixed a big bowl of lemonade with ice cubes. Philip picked a spot under the maple tree and waited for customers. In just a few minutes the mailman stopped and bought two glasses. Then a grandpa and grandma came along. Soon Philip's lemonade bowl was empty, but his pockets were heavy with coins. They made lots of

FRESH
Lemonade
10¢ A CUP

clinks as they went into the piggy bank.

Philip worked hard all week. Every day more coins clinked into the piggy bank. There were even some poofs as dollar bills softly tumbled in. On Saturday Philip took all the money out of the bank and counted it. And was he surprised! There was more than enough money to buy the pole Philip wanted.

"Dad! Dad!" Philip called. "I can buy my own pole now."

"I'm proud of you, Philip," Dad said as he gave Philip a big hug.

Philip and Tippy ran all the way to the store. After they paid for the fishing pole, they stopped to get a big ice cream cone. But before Philip was able to take a lick,
PLOP!!!
the ice cream fell on the ground. Tippy made a dive for it.

Philip giggled, "Oh, well, Tippy, I guess we both got something special today."

Tippy looked up
and smiled.
And Philip had a
big smile, too.

Brian's Bear

Little Brian had a very best friend—a soft brown bear named Teddy. Every night Brian would pick up Teddy, climb the stairs, and get into bed. When Mom came in for a good-night kiss, Brian would hold up Teddy and say, "Teddy wants a kiss, too, Mom."

Brian and Teddy did everything to-

gether. When Brian went to the park, so did Teddy. When Brian went to the store,

Teddy came along and they rode side-by-side in the grocery cart. When Brian ate lunch, Teddy ate lunch.

Brian had a five-year-old cousin named Andy. One day Andy asked Brian to spend the night at his house. Brian was very excited and the first thing he packed was Teddy.

Brian and Andy had lots of fun. They laughed and played. All the while, Teddy was close by, watching and smiling. The boys told funny stories until way past their bedtime.

The next morning the boys jumped out of bed and ran downstairs to quickly eat breakfast and get ready to play.

The next thing they knew, Brian's mom came to pick him up. Brian ran upstairs to get Teddy. He had left him in the chair by the bed because Teddy looked so sleepy that morning. He wasn't used to sleeping in a strange house and really needed a morning nap.

Brian came running down the steps. He was crying big, big tears.

"Mom, Teddy's gone. I can't find him anywhere. He's just disappeared."

Everyone in the house looked for Teddy. They looked behind the chairs, under the bed, on all the shelves. They even looked

in the waste baskets. No Teddy, any-where! Then they looked in the backyard. No Teddy. There was only one place left, the front yard. They looked under every bush and behind every tree. Still no Teddy.

Brian went up to the bedroom again to see if Teddy was there. He was still crying big tears. Andy was waiting for him.

"Brian, I have something to tell you," Andy said quietly. "I'm really sorry that I made you cry."

Brian wiped his eyes. "Oh, you didn't make me sad, Andy. I'm just sad because I can't find my Teddy."

Andy looked down at his feet. "But I know where Teddy is," he said. "I didn't mean to make you cry. I have never had a bear before and I didn't think you would miss him that much. I'm really sorry, Brian." And Andy began to cry.

Brian gave Andy a hug and for a few

minutes the cousins cried together. Then
Andy went to the closet, pushed the shoes
out of the way, pulled
out a box from the
corner, and lifted
Teddy out of his
hiding place.

"Here he is, Brian. I did a bad thing when I took Teddy and hid him. I'm sorry. I feel so sad." Andy cried a few more tears—and these were VERY BIG TEARS. He even sobbed a few times and just kept his head down.

"That's OK, Andy, I know you didn't do it to make me sad," Brian said as he hugged Teddy.

Andy tried hard to stop crying.

Brian reached over to pat Andy's shoulder. Then he smiled and said, "I've got a good idea. Just wait here, Andy, and I'll be back in a minute."

In a few minutes Brian came back with a sheet of paper folded to make a small square. On the outside it said:

To Andy
from
Your friend Brian

Andy carefully unfolded the paper. There was a drawing of a teddy bear.

"I wish this was a real bear, Andy," Brian said, "but at least you can keep this picture until you have your very own teddy bear."

Andy giggled, "Oh, thank you, Brian. I may not need a real teddy bear. I like this picture because you made it to help me feel better."

That night when he went to bed, Andy asked his dad to hang the drawing of the teddy bear above his bed. Before he went to sleep, Andy looked up at his teddy bear and said, "Night, Teddy, I'm so glad you came to live with me."

Cindy's Day at the Zoo

"Are you ready, Cindy?" asked Mother. "Today is zoo day, remember?"

"Sure, Mom, I've been ready for hours—at least for ten minutes," Cindy called.

So off they went. Cindy was so excited. She was going to see live animals—lots of them.

Mom and Cindy stopped to buy pink cotton candy, and Cindy held the candy close to her mouth (but not in front of her eyes) as she and Mom stopped to look at the elephants.

One elephant was grabbing dirt with his long trunk and throwing it on his back. It looked as though a sandbox had fallen from the sky and landed there. Cindy imagined she was playing on the elephant's back. What a wonderful place to play!

The zoo keeper came and put out some hay for the elephants to eat. As they curled the hay in their trunks, the elephants snorted. Cindy was sure that was their way of thanking the zoo keeper for their food. The zoo keeper nodded and tipped his cap at the elephants and then went on to feed the bears. Cindy and her mom followed.

It was a hot day and another worker was spraying the bears with a hose. The bears were running through the water just like children play around a sprinkler. Suddenly one of the bears ran toward a big pool and jumped in. Splash!!!

Splish!!!! Splat!!!! water flew everywhere. The zoo keeper had water dripping off his nose and eyelashes. There were even some drops on his ears. He was soaked! Cindy and the other zoo visitors laughed. The bear had a twinkle in his eye. Cindy was sure the bear did that on purpose!

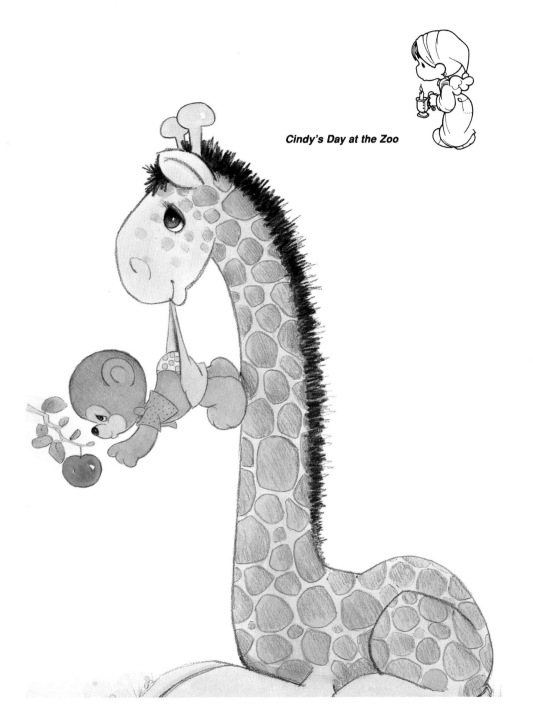

Next, they saw a giraffe helping his small bear cub friend take an apple off a nearby tree.

Cindy and her mom went on and on, visiting all the animals. Finally, at the end of the day they found the seals. The zoo keeper was feeding them some small fish. He would toss a fish in the water and the seals would dive under water to get it. Some of the seals tossed the fish in the air and others clapped, just to thank the zoo keeper for feeding them. Cindy could see how much the zoo keeper and the seals liked each other.

On the ride home, Cindy thought about her day at the zoo. She learned that animals need love and care and patience, just as people do. Soon Cindy's eyes were closed. She was dreaming of the day when she could be a zoo keeper. She wondered which animal she would like to feed first. Maybe the elephant—no, the bears were lots of fun. But the seals were the best of all.

Suddenly she sat up. "Mom, I have a question."

"Yes, dear," Mom replied.

"How could Noah get all those animals in a boat? That's just so hard to believe."

Mom smiled gently at Cindy. "I have a question for you, too. Look out the window and up at the sky. Do you see all those stars and planets in the sky? Just look—there's the moon and Jupiter and Pluto and Mars."

Cindy looked and looked. "Jupiter? The

moon? Stars? I don't see anything but the blue sky, Mom."

"Well, yes, that's true, Cindy," Mother said. "I don't see the planets either. But I know they're there. In fact, the Bible says that they've been up there ever since God made them and placed them there. If he placed all those planets and stars in the heavens, then it was no problem for him to fit all those animals on Noah's boat."

"Even the elephants?" Cindy asked.

"Even the elephants," Mother smiled. "You see, Cindy, faith is believing or trusting that what God says is true."

"I'm so glad we went to the zoo today, Mom. I learned a special lesson. I don't have to see everything to believe it. God can do anything. He made all the animals and he can fit a whole zoo full of animals on one boat.

Sticky Fingerprints

"Sure hope Mom doesn't catch me," Peter mumbled as he sneaked out the back door. "If she finds out that I took some jelly doughnuts, I'll be in real TROUBLE." He tiptoed across the back porch and spied his friend Dutch waiting around the corner of the house.

Family Times

"Mmmmm!" said Dutch. "Those look yummy."

"But you can't eat them here," scolded

118

Peter. "We have to eat these someplace where Mom won't find us."

"But I'm hungry," complained Dutch.

"Just wait," Peter whispered impatiently. "We have to find the right place."

Peter tried to think. Dutch just licked his chubby chops and tried not to drool. Those doughnuts were made for eating and he wanted a bite NOW.

"That's it. The car will be the perfect spot. Mom won't be using it today because she has to stay home with Grandpa."

"Let's open the door and get in," said Dutch with a silly grin on his face.

Soon Peter and Dutch were snuggled in the front seat of the car enjoying their jelly doughnuts. Peter giggled as he munched bite after bite. Jelly oozed between his fingers and even dribbled down his face. One swipe with his right sleeve smeared jelly all over his chin.

"Isn't this great?" he said. "Mom will

never know we took these doughnuts. She made so many, I'm sure she didn't count them."

"Look at our hands," Dutch said as he squeezed the jelly between his fingers. "This is so gooey and so much fun, why don't you go and get some more?"

Suddenly the front door opened and Mom headed toward the car.

"Yikes!!! It's Mom!" Peter cried. "Let's sneak out on your side. But don't make ANY noise!"

The neighbor across the street called to Mom and she turned to talk to him. Very quietly two sticky boys opened the car door, slid to the ground, carefully closed the door, and crawled to the other side of the garage.

"Phew! that was close," said Dutch.

"Yeah, too close," agreed Peter. "C'mon, let's clean our hands with the hose."

The next morning Peter and his dad sat

at the kitchen table while Mom served the eggs. After they had eaten, Mom took a tray of jelly doughnuts from the warming oven.

"Surprise!" she said as she handed one to Dad. "How about you, Peter? Would you like one, too?"

Peter felt warm and hot and cold all at the same time. He felt like squirming on his chair and his stomach was taking flip-flops. He was feeling VERY GUILTY. But he tried his best to cover up.

"Thanks, Mom. They look yummy!" Peter said.

"And they *are* yummy," Dad said as he took a big bite. "I don't think I've ever tasted one of these. Is this a new recipe?"

"Hmm-mm, that's very strange," said Mom. "Are you sure you've never eaten one of these?" she asked Dad as she looked directly at him.

"Absolutely sure," said Dad. "I would

have remembered eating something as good as this."

"And what about you, Peter? Have you ever eaten one?" asked Mom.

"Not that I know of," stammered Peter. He was getting hot and cold again. And his stomach was really jumping.

"Then I wonder whose sticky fingerprints were on the door handles of my car. And who left clumps of sticky jelly on the seat covers?" asked Mom.

"Oh, Mom," cried Peter as he got off his chair and went to hug her, "I thought you'd never find out. You made so many I was sure you'd never miss a couple. I'm really sorry that I took the doughnuts without asking and then lied about taking them."

Mom and Dad could see that Peter was really sorry. They saw the tears and his sad face. But Peter had to learn his les-

son, so they let him feel sad for a few minutes. Soon he was sobbing.

Then Mom said, "Peter, I forgive you. You see, when you do wrong things, you are sinning. The Bible says that our sins have a way of uncovering themselves. You may think you have them hidden but soon they pop up and make you feel sad. Let's ask God to forgive you, too."

"I really learned a lesson," Peter said softly.

"Good for you, Son, said Dad. "I'm sure this doughnut will taste even better than the ones you ate yesterday."

Chopsticks

Four-year-old Ruben loved to play the piano. Because Ruben's parents didn't have enough money to buy a piano, Ruben would often go to his aunt's house to play her piano. He didn't know how to play real songs so he just made up tunes as he played on the keys.

"It will be nice when you are old enough

to go to school," Ruben's mother said. "They have a piano at school and maybe when you are in the second grade you can take music lessons there."

Ruben liked school and he liked almost all of his classmates, but the thing he LOVED most of all was the big piano in the auditorium. He often asked his teacher for permission to stay after class and play that big piano.

One day when Ruben came into the auditorium an older student was playing a tune.

Ruben listened quietly. "What's that song?" he asked.

"Chopsticks," the older boy answered.

"Will you teach me how to play it?" Ruben asked.

"Sure, it's easy," the boy replied. "Just put your hand here and follow me."

Ruben watched carefully. Together they played the tune several times. When

the older boy left, Ruben practiced over and over until he memorized each note. Finally he knew a real song to play on the piano. Ruben couldn't wait to get home to tell his parents.

"Father," Ruben said, "I learned to play a real song on the piano. I practiced and practiced and now I know each note by heart."

"That's wonderful, Ruben," said Father. "But now you must get ready for dinner because Mother has a surprise for you as soon as we are finished eating."

Ruben hardly said a word while he was eating. All he

could think of was the song he had learned that day. He was trying hard not to forget a single note.

"Ruben, you are so quiet," his mother said. "Don't you want to know what your surprise is going to be?"

Ruben almost jumped. "Oh, Mother, I was thinking about the song I learned. I just can't think about anything else. I finally know how to play a real song on the piano!"

Mother smiled as she held two tickets in her hand. "Do you know what I have here?" she asked.

"Looks like tickets to me," replied Ruben.

"That's right," Mother answered. "The great Podrinski is going to give a concert at the Music Center tonight. He is one of the best pianists in the world and you and I are going to hear him."

Ruben's eyes grew very large as he

looked at the two tickets. "Can we leave right now, Mother? I want to be there first so we can sit down near the piano."

Ruben and his mother left early to be sure that they would get the best seats.

"You're much too early," the doorman scolded and he would not let them go inside. Ruben was so excited that the doorman finally let them in.

"Just be careful, Ruben. I'm not allowed to let people in this early. Don't get into trouble," the doorman warned them.

Ruben promised. Mother promised. So they both went way down to the front, close to the piano. Ruben settled back and tried to remember all the notes to the song he learned that day. Soon other people came and the auditorium lights began to dim. It was almost time for the concert to begin.

"I'm glad we came early, Ruben," said Mother as she turned to look at her son.

But Ruben wasn't there. His seat was empty.

"Oh, dear! Where is Ruben?" gasped Mother.

Suddenly the velvet curtains lifted, a spotlight came on, and a man walked on stage.

"Ladies and gentlemen," he said, "I would like to introduce the great Podrinski!"

The audience cheered, the spotlight was turned to the piano, and. . . there sat little Ruben. He didn't notice anything at all. He was playing his song on the big piano.

"This is TERRIBLE!!!" one of the stage crew whispered. "Where did that little boy come from?"

"Just get him AWAY from that piano and OFF the stage RIGHT NOW!!!" another demanded.

The audience was in complete shock as

Chopsticks

Ruben carefully played one note after another. Suddenly someone stepped into the spotlight and sat down gently next to Ruben. He listened quietly until Ruben finished his song.

"What are you playing?" he asked Ruben.

"Chopsticks," said Ruben. And he started to play the song again.

"I know the harmony part to that song. Let's play it together. I'll play my part and you can play the notes you know. OK, let's start over: one, two, three," said the kind gentleman.

The man lovingly placed one hand on Ruben's shoulder and together they played "Chopsticks." When they were finished, the man asked Ruben to stand and take a bow. There was a thunderous applause from the audience. Then the stage crew quickly took charge and Ruben went back to his seat.

"Mother, why are there tears in your eyes?" Ruben asked.

"Oh, Ruben," she said, "do you know that you just played a duet with the great Podrinski? He was so kind to you. You're too young now to know what a special thing he did for you. But never forget how kind the great Podrinski was to you to-night. I hope that when you grow up you'll be as kind to young children as he was to you."

3 *Animal*
Tales

Me First

Rollie was a little bear who had to be first. He ALWAYS had to be first. If he was second or third, he would push his way up to the front of the line. He would push hard with his sharp elbows or give a mean shove with his shoulders.

When it was time to eat, Rollie AL-WAYS took the biggest piece. Rollie

ALWAYS helped himself first, even if his grandmother was eating with them and should have had first choice.

Rollie never shared anything—his toys, his food, or his very favorite bike. He always wanted first turn, or to be first at bat if he was playing ball. Rollie was a VERY GREEDY bear. He was not fun to be with.

One day Teddy Bear came rushing over to his friends, "C'mon!!! I've found a honey tree. It's the biggest one I've ever seen. And this is how I found it."

Of course, Rollie couldn't wait to hear the details. He waited until the others were busy talking and then ZOOM!! Rollie quietly sneaked away. He had heard just enough to find the tree and, of course, he ALWAYS had to be the first one. So when the friends got to the big tree on the hill, there was no honey, none at all. Just a very sticky Rollie.

Another day, Panda Bear came running up to the bear friends. "C'mon!!! I've just found the biggest blackberry bush in the valley. It's not far from the big pine tree. C'mon!!! I'll show you where it is."

Again, Rollie did not wait for the details. He ran as fast as his bear legs would

141

carry him. He was out of breath when he found the blackberry bush, but that didn't stop him from pushing one berry after another in his mouth. The friends made a lot of noise scrambling through the valley but when they saw Rollie, they didn't make any noise at all. They were very quiet. Rollie had a very purple face. He had eaten all the blackberries. There wasn't even one blackberry left.

The bear friends were sitting in the sun one day when Teddy came rushing up over the hill. "C'mon!!! I know where there's a great fishing hole. It's just past the bend in the river. I just saw the biggest fish ever there!"

Would you like to guess what Rollie did? You're right. He took off for the fishing hole without waiting for the other friends. He ALWAYS had to be first.

When the bear friends rounded the

bend they saw a very unhappy Rollie. He was crying. And he didn't have any fish, either.

"What happened to you, Rollie?" asked Teddy.

Rollie wiped his eyes. "I tried to catch the biggest fish in the river. But it turned out not to be a fish at all. It was a very snappy turtle. It bit me right on the tail," Rollie sobbed.

"And that's not all, either," Rollie cried. "A big bee stung me right on the shoulder. I'm hurting all over!"

"But I knew that turtle was there, Rollie. If you had waited for us, we could have helped you and you probably wouldn't have a turtle bite and a bee sting," said Teddy.

Rollie sobbed, "If only I hadn't been so greedy. I think I've learned my lesson today. Will you still be my friends? I'll try

hard not to be first all the time. But will you let me be first once in a while?"

The friends gave Rollie a big bear hug. They were glad not to have a GREEDY Rollie anymore.

Little Mouse

Little Mouse lived in the sugar bowl on the bottom shelf of Mrs. Nagel's kitchen cupboard. He loved his home because Mrs. Nagel was such a nice lady. She always made sure Little Mouse had lots of cheese and crackers to eat. And she was quiet when Little Mouse was sleeping. Once he took a nap on a shelf. He was

sleeping so soundly that he didn't hear any sounds when Mrs. Nagel came with a paintbrush to paint the shelf. She quietly painted one end of the shelf, then the other. Little Mouse slept on. She painted above him. She painted below him. Little Mouse didn't stir. She finally had to stop painting because Little Mouse kept on sleeping. Mrs. Nagel was too kind to wake him up.

But Mr. Nagel was not quiet. Mr. Nagel did not like Little Mouse. He would yell at Little Mouse and throw things at him. If he saw Little Mouse run across the floor, Mr. Nagel would jump on a chair. He even put mouse traps in the cupboards! Little Mouse had to be careful when he scampered through the cupboards. One day he was going so fast that SNAP! the tip of Little Mouse's tail was caught in the trap. Little Mouse cried and howled. But they

were only tiny noises because a mouse is not very big.

Mrs. Nagel heard Little Mouse's tiny noises. She lifted him out of the trap, bandaged his tail, put him in his sugar bowl, and gave him some cheese.

"Stay in the bowl and rest, Little Mouse," she said. "You'll feel better in the morning."

Mrs. Nagel was right. Little Mouse's tail did not hurt the next morning. But Little Mouse was still sad. You see, his heart hurt because Mr. Nagel did not like him.

Little Mouse wondered about that problem all day. He wondered so hard that he was very tired at night. He still didn't have an answer but thought there was nothing better to do but go to sleep.

Little Mouse was asleep only a short time when his nose began to twitch. It twitched and twitched. Little Mouse

Little Mouse

rubbed his paw over his nose but then he sat up straight. "I smell something. Something is hurting my nose. I think that is SMOKE."

Sure enough, when Little Mouse jumped out of his sugar-bowl home, onto the shelf, and then found his favorite track down to the floor, he knew there was smoke he saw some FLAMES coming out of the stove.

"Oh, dear!!! Oh, dear!!! Oh, dear!!!" said Little Mouse. He would have said some more Oh-dears but there wasn't any time to lose. He ran to the bedroom and climbed up to where Mr. and Mrs. Nagel were sleeping. They were sound asleep. They didn't know their house was burning. Little Mouse jumped down on Mrs. Nagel's arm. She woke up.

"Little Mouse, Little Mouse! What are you doing here?" she cried. She was very surprised and still much too sleepy to

151

smell smoke. Little Mouse ran up her arm and down her arm again, just to be sure she would really wake up.

Mrs. Nagel sat up. "George!!! Wake up! Wake up NOW!!! I smell smoke. Let's call the fire department and get out of here."

They both quickly climbed out of bed, called the fire department, and ran outside.

The firemen worked hard to put out the fire.

"There is only a little damage to your kitchen, Mrs. Nagel. How did you wake up in time?" the fire chief asked.

Mrs. Nagel smiled. Mr. Nagel smiled. He picked up Little Mouse. "A little friend warned us," Mr. Nagel said.

Little Mouse was so happy to hear Mr. Nagel call him a friend. Little Mouse wouldn't have to worry about traps in the cupboard anymore. In fact, Mr. Nagel

Little Mouse

gave Little Mouse a tiny little mouse hug before he put him back in the sugar bowl.

Little Mouse was a happy mouse, and he was home to stay.

Leo's Birthday

Today is Leo's birthday. He is five years old today. All his life he had lived at the circus. When he was a little cub, crowds of people would come to see him puff out his chest and try to roar. It wasn't a roar at all, just a soft, baby noise. But Leo grew and grew. Soon he had big teeth and could ROAR like a big lion. But all the people

knew Leo had a soft heart and was just acting. When the crowds went home, Leo would roll over and purr until someone rubbed his big furry tummy. Everyone loved Leo.

Leo's friend Duncan was so sad. "Today is Leo's birthday," he said. "And I don't have a present for him. I wanted to make something nice. All I have are some tools and an old rug. I can't make a present out of that."

Leo's other friend Bambi

was also sad. He said, "Today is Leo's birthday. And I don't have a present for him. I wanted to make something nice, but all I have is some boards and paint. I can't make a present out of this."

Duncan heard Bambi's sad story. "Let's cooperate," said Duncan.

"What's cooperate?" asked Bambi.

"It's when we work together to get something done," Duncan said. "If we put our stuff together, we can make some-

159

thing much nicer than we could make alone."

Duncan and Bambi decided to cooperate. Bambi held the boards while Duncan sawed them. Bambi brushed pretty red paint on the boards while Duncan held the paint can. And while Duncan was putting his rug on the new floor, Bambi was hanging curtains in the window.

When they were finished, Duncan and Bambi stood back.

"That's a beautiful lion house!" Bambi said.

"We did it right because we worked together," Duncan replied.

And the two happy friends went off to find Leo. They made him shut his eyes as they led him toward the present they had made.

"OK, now you may open your eyes," Bambi said. "Turn around, Leo. Here's a

present we made for your fifth birthday.
We wanted to make something special for
you."

Animal Tales

"Wow!!!" said Leo. "My very own lion house. And you painted it my favorite color. This is the best present I ever had. Thanks, friends. You made my day."

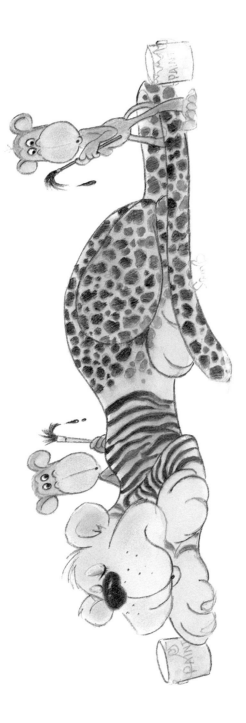

4 *School*
Days

Marcia's Beautiful Voice

Marcia had a beautiful voice. But Marcia had a problem. She was TOO PROUD of her beautiful voice.

"My, you have a nice voice, Marcia," her friends would say.

"I know it," Marcia would reply. "I'm going to be the world's best singer."

One day Marcia's friends were reading a poster in the school hallway.

"What's that all about?" Marcia asked.

"Oh, Marcia," Mary replied, "there's going to be a singing contest tomorrow night. You'll just have to be there."

"Is that so? I'll probably win the contest because I'm the best singer around, but I guess I could enter," Marcia quipped.

During class the music teacher asked Bryan to hand out yellow cards with the contest rules. When he offered Marcia one, she turned up her nose and said. "I don't need one of those stupid cards! Everyone knows that I have the best voice. I'm going to win that contest without even trying to."

"Why didn't you take the rule card, Marcia?" Tammy asked as they waited their turn to perform. "Some of the rules weren't about singing."

"Who needs rules?" snapped Marcia. "Rules are made for people who can't sing."

"Well, here I go," said Tammy. "I'll do my best but I don't think I'm going to win."

"I hope you have just a short song to sing," snapped Marcia. "This contest is taking so-o-oo long."

Marcia was last in line and was very impatient about waiting for her turn.

"Will that Jenny ever finish?" she complained. "Just listen to her! How did she ever get into this contest with a crummy voice like that?"

"Jenny has a nice voice," Tammy argued.

"Well, of course, *you* would think so," snapped Marcia. "After all, you never had a voice lesson in your life."

After waiting for a very long time, Marcia was called to center stage. *I'm*

terrific! she thought to herself as she sang
with her nose high in the air.

"You were wonderful," said Tammy.

"It's like they always say," Marcia boasted. "We save the best for last."

"Well, I think you should tell Jenny that you're sorry you said she had a crummy voice," insisted Tammy.

"OK, I'm sorry that your voice is crummy, Jenny," Marcia laughed as she looked at Jenny.

Tears ran down Jenny's cheeks. Marcia just chuckled again.

Suddenly the music teacher walked on stage. Everyone, except Marcia, wondered who the winner would be. Marcia knew that Marcia would win.

"Ladies and gentlemen, we have a winner. Jenny Bronson, will you please come up?" said the teacher.

The audience clapped loudly.

Marcia gasped and looked at Jenny with surprise.

"As you know," the teacher continued, "to be a great singer one must have more than just a nice voice. One must have a friendly smile and poise and a pleasing personality. Jenny meets all of these qualifications. Congratulations, Jenny! You are the winner."

The audience clapped again. Jenny smiled and smiled. No one noticed that there were dried tears on her cheeks.

"Where's Marcia?" Jenny asked as soon as she joined her friends.

"I think she found the losers' corner," Tammy quipped.

"Let's go find her," said Jenny. "She must be feeling very sad."

"Marcia, I'm so sorry," Jenny said when she found Marcia. "I know you were counting on winning."

"I'm sorry, too," cried Marcia. "But not because I lost, Jenny. I'm sorry because I was so proud and so mean to you. I'm

172

going to try to have a beautiful personality like you do. That's more important than having a beautiful voice."

And all the friends clapped loudly as Jenny put her arms around her friend Marcia.

REPORT CARD
Kindness .. A
Mercy .... A
Love ... A
faithfullness A

teacher

Being Different Is Special

Jim waved good-bye to his school friends as his mother drove up in the station wagon.

"How was school today?" Mother asked as she pulled away from the curb.

"OK. I did really good on my science test." Jim showed her the paper with the happy face drawn on it.

"Very good, Son, an A! I'm proud of you and Dad will be, too. Anything else happen today?"

"Well, we played kick ball at recess time. That was a blast!"

Mother laughed as she looked at the dirt on Jim's jeans. "I can see that you had a lot of fun."

"Yeah, we sure did, all of us except Michael."

"Who is Michael?" Mother asked.

"He's a new boy at school. Some of the kids were making fun of him and he started crying."

"Why were the other kids picking on him?" Mother asked.

"He has to use crutches. Sometimes he needs help walking."

"Jim, I want to ask you something. What kind of a boy do you think Michael would be if he didn't need crutches?"

Jim thought for a minute as he looked out the window. "Just like the rest of us, I guess."

"Now, what if your legs didn't work right? What if they were weak and you had to use crutches?" asked Mother.

"Well, my legs might be weak, but I would have strong arms and eyes and ears and my brain would be like anyone else's."

"How about your feelings, Jim? Would you like to have people tease you about your weak legs? Or to laugh at you because you walked differently?"

"No, Mom, I wouldn't."

Mother smiled at Jim and said, "Every-one of us is a little bit different."

"I'm glad we're different, Mom. I mean, you like to grow flowers and bake cookies. I like to eat cookies and watch the stars and planets."

"It wouldn't be very much fun if we were

all the same," agreed Mother. "Being different makes you special. And you are very special, Jim. So is Michael."

"Now I know why Michael cried," Jim said. "He's just like the rest of us, except for his legs. Some people have weak eyes, or weak ears. But that doesn't give us the right to tease them."

"Right, Son," said Mother. "Some people can't hear well, some people have trouble talking clearly. Some people can't walk. Some people can't see. We are all different, each of us in our own way."

Jim thought about that for a minute or two. Suddenly he turned to Mother and said, "Stop, Mom. There's Michael now. He sure looks sad climbing those steps. I'll see if he can come over to our house. Tom and John are coming to work on pinebox derby cars. Michael can make one, too."

"Hey, Michael!" Jim called. "Can you

come over and work on pinebox derby cars? Tom and John are coming, too. We can have a mock race as soon as we're finished."

Michael smiled as he shuffled over to the car. "I'd like that, Jim. Last year I made a couple of cars and almost won the derby. I think if I make one or two changes, I'll have a sure winner this time."

"Good," said Jim. "See you soon. You can probably give us some good tips because this is our first year in the derby."

As he turned to his mom, Jim said, "Let's get going. I hope you have lots of chocolate chip cookies, Mom, because derby racers get really hungry!"

Clown School

Did you know that clowns have to go to school to learn how to juggle, and balance, and put on their sad or happy faces?

Boomer and Taffy had been clowns for a long time and now they were teachers at the Happy Day Clown School.

"Boomer!" Taffy called. "You'd better

hurry. You don't want to be late for the first day of school."

Boomer grabbed his lunch box and hurried after his friend. "I wonder what kind of clowns we'll have to teach this year," he said.

Taffy laughed. "Well, they can't be as bad as last year's clowns! Do you remember little Flip and his Amazing Wonder Dog? Flip tried everything to get that puppy to do his tricks. And then there was Top-

186

per, the world's clumsiest clown! He wanted to be a juggler but the balls kept landing on his head."

"And who could forget little Beanie?" giggled Boomer. "She wanted to be the best roller skating clown ever.

The only problem was that she couldn't stay up for more than two minutes. By the end of the third week we had pillows tied all over her to keep her safe."

Taffy giggled again. "Do you remember Lolly and Pop, her goose? Lolly tried to train that silly thing to walk the tightrope, but all the goose wanted to do was eat her bows and ribbons. Wasn't Lolly surprised when Pop turned out to be the best high diver the circus ever had?"

"Yes," said Boomer, "Lolly turned out to be a very good tightrope walker! I think that's what I like best about being a teacher. We start out every year with a bunch of little clowns who fall all over each other trying to be the best clown. But by the end of the year the little clowns realize that when they work together and help each other, each clown can discover what he or she can do the best."

"That's right," Taffy agreed. "When Flip tried to teach Topper how to juggle without dropping the balls, Flip discovered he could catch just about anything. Now Flip is our best juggler."

"And if Topper didn't try to help Beanie learn to balance," said Boomer, "Topper wouldn't have discovered how good he is on the unicycle. I don't think I've ever seen anyone who can do the tricks he does. . . and he was our clumsiest clown."

As Boomer and Taffy walked through the school gates, they saw all kinds of little clowns tumbling and falling all over each other.

"Oh, well," Boomer laughed, "here we go again."

The Faker

"I don't like school!" Timmy groaned as he turned over in bed. He stuck a fever thermometer in his mouth, hoping he was sick.

"Shucks, no fever today," sighed Timmy. "Guess I'll have to get up."

Timmy stomped out of the bedroom. Then he tramped down the steps, plunk,

plunk!! PLUNK!!!! And he was just as noisy coming into the kitchen. He got himself some juice out of the refrigerator.

He grumped at the refrigerator, snarled at the stove, and glared at the bread dough and flour on the kitchen counter. He really did like Mom's home-made bread, but he was much too crabby to think about that.

Seeing all that white flour on the counter gave Timmy an idea. It was such a good idea that he almost smiled.

"Let's see, if I plan this right, I won't have to go to school today," Timmy said aloud to no one in particular.

Timmy sneaked over to the counter, picked up two handfuls of flour, and rubbed the flour all over his face. He didn't notice that he had a collar of white flour and smears of white flour all over his arms. There was even a clump or two of flour in his hair.

"Wow! I must really look sick now."

A few minutes later, Timmy's mother walked into the room. She saw Timmy holding his stomach and moaning. She also saw the clumps of flour in Timmy's hair and the smears of flour on his cheeks and chin. Mother covered up a smile and tried to look sad.

"Oh, Timmy!" Mother cried. "What is wrong with you?"

"I'm so sick this morning, Mom, that I just can't even think of going to school," Timmy groaned.

"Well, I had better get your father!" Mother cried.

When Timmy's father saw how white he was, he shook his head sadly. "Poor, poor Timmy!" he said.

"Poor Timmy is sick," his mother said, trying to hide her smile. "Look at how white he is. Do you think he has the flu?"

"How horrible! How sad!" Father said.

"Maybe you should cook some eggs and send him back to bed as soon as he is finished eating. You know," his father continued, "I once read that eggs with plenty of pepper is the best thing to cure the flu."

"That's true," said Mother as she put two eggs on Timmy's plate.

"And now for the best part," Father said as he secretly winked at Mother.

Father took the pepper shaker and began to cover Timmy's eggs with pepper. All at once, Timmy's nose began to twitch and he let out a great big sneeze.

"Ker-choo!"
"KER-CHOO-OO!!!"

Flour flew in all directions and began to settle on the kitchen floor.

Timmy's face no longer was white. Even the clumps of flour in his hair had

disappeared. There were only a few streaks of flour on his shoulders, and they didn't make Timmy look at all sick.

"Well, what do you know? It worked," Timmy's father laughed. "Now, Timmy, it looks like all the flu bugs have left. You just lost your excuse for missing school today."

Timmy's face turned all shades of red. He was so ashamed that he forgot to feel sorry that his trick didn't work.

Father said, "There is a verse in the Bible that says, 'Be sure your sin will find you out.' That verse means that sooner or later the wrong things that we do will be discovered and then we will be sorry that we sinned. And I would say that your little plan to stay home from school didn't work, Tim."

Timmy gulped. "But your trick on me worked, didn't it?"

Mother smiled as she dusted the flour

from Timmy's pajama top. "You know," she said, "Father and I knew what you were up to, Timmy. But rather than talking to you or scolding you about it, we wanted to find out if our trick would teach you a lesson you wouldn't forget."

"It sure was a good lesson, Mom. I'm sorry that I tried to trick you."

"And now that you are feeling so much better, don't you think it's time to get ready for school?" Mother suggested.

Field Day

"Oh, boy!!! Today is Field Day," yelled Ricky as he climbed out of bed. He was excited about the big race. He always won and that made him very happy.

There were races, long jumps, and all sorts of other sports on Field Day. Ricky's friends were going to be in the races, too. And parents and grandparents always

came. There were lots of people to cheer and lots of people to hug the winners. Sometimes grandmas and grandpas had to comfort the losers, but Ricky didn't even want to think about that.

Ricky got to school early that day. Kids were on the playground and teachers began to line up the children so Field Day could begin.

The first event was the softball throw. Girls and boys threw softballs as far as they could, and the teachers measured how far each ball went.

Ricky's friend Jimmy had thrown the best toss so far. Now it was Ricky's turn. His teacher handed him the softball. The ball felt good in his hand. He

looked at Mom and Dad and smiled. Then he wound up and th-r-e-w-w-w with all his might. Never had Ricky thrown a ball so far. It sailed through the air and landed with a hard thud. His classmates cheered. Ricky had thrown the ball beyond the mark made by Jimmy. Ricky won that toss, but not by much.

Next came the broad jump. They stood at the line and jumped as far as they could. One by one the children lined up and jumped. Sure enough, Jimmy jumped way beyond everyone else. It looked like Jimmy was going to win this one. Now it was Ricky's turn. He jumped farther than anyone else, just a little bit farther than Jimmy did. So Ricky won that contest. And Jimmy came in second.

The final event of the day was the 50-yard dash. This was the most important race. And, of course, Ricky wanted to win. So did Jimmy. The friends looked at each

other and smiled. Each knew that the other one could beat him. But both of them were going to try hard to win.

"On your mark!"

"Get set!"

"GO-o-o-oo!"

Ricky quickly took the lead, running as fast as his legs could carry him. The others fell behind, except for Jimmy, who was running very fast, too. Suddenly the friends were even. The two best friends were tied with only a few more feet to go. They were huffing and puffing! Everyone was cheering them on. Then Jimmy took the lead. Jimmy had won! Jimmy had finally won a race. He just smiled and smiled. Then, with his hands high in the air, he began jumping up and down with happiness!!!

But Ricky, who had never lost a race, wasn't happy at all. He was very UN-happy. He began to cry.

"I'm sorry, Mom and Dad," Ricky whimpered.

"Son, there is nothing to be sorry about," said his father. "You did a fine job."

"Sure," his mother agreed. "You've had your day in the sun, which is more than some people ever get."

Ricky looked at his mom and said, "What do you mean by 'day in the sun,' Mom?"

"You've won many events and most people don't win even one. Finishing second isn't bad. You don't have to feel sorry about that. The idea is to have fun and be happy for the winner."

"You're right, Mom," said Ricky. "I've got to go over and congratulate Jim now."

Both of the best-friend winners had big smiles.

"Congratulations, Jim. You're the best!" said Ricky.

"Congratulations yourself, Ricky. I think you're the best," said Jim.

And the best friends went off the field together, arms around each other's shoulders.

5 *Sleepytime Stories*

Sweet Dreams

Tommy said his prayers and climbed into bed. His mom had told him to think of nice things before he went to sleep so he could have sweet dreams.

With a big smile on his face, Tommy stretched out, put his hands under his head, and said, "Let's see, what's the first thing I want to do tomorrow?"

It was butterfly time where Tommy lived. Maybe Tommy and his friend Scott could watch the butterflies in the open field next to Tommy's house. Scott and Tommy together  had counted over a hundred butterflies there yesterday.

"Just think," said Scott. "These butterflies used to be yukky caterpillars. Now they're flying fast through the air. They've forgotten about being caterpillars."

Tommy's eyes began to close. He dreamed he was a butterfly and the soft wind was carrying him across the field. Whoops!! he landed on a mushroom, a blue one!

Tommy was growing tired of being on the mushroom. *Maybe I'll turn myself back into Tommy and watch the ants for a while. I just love to see them scurrying around. They're always so-oo-o busy.* So he headed for the big anthill. Tommy's mother had told him that ants were the strongest insects in the world. He believed that, because he watched them carry sand around. They were hurrying around the anthill, each one busy doing his job. Tommy stayed for about ten minutes and then decided he had watched the ants long enough.

Dianne, Tommy's sister, had found some baby birds that day. She even held one that had fallen from its nest. But, of course, Dianne wouldn't let Tommy hold it. She was the big sister and Tommy was only a little boy—much too little to know how to hold a baby bird!

Hah!!! Now I'll be able to hold that little bird. Maybe I can even hold two birds! Tommy was really having a good dream this time. When Tommy finally found the nest, Mama Bird was guarding the two little ones and wouldn't let Tommy get near them, not even in his dream.

Now what will I dream about? Hmmm, I'm beginning to smell pancakes and bacon and yummy cinnamon rolls. I sure hope this isn't a dream—because I'm very hungry.

"Tommy! Tommy! It's time to get up! Breakfast is ready and waiting," called Mother. "Did you have sweet dreams last night?"

What do you think Tommy said?

A Night in Letter Land

Benji didn't like to do his homework, and he especially hated to work on spelling. He thought it was silly to learn how to make the letters of the alphabet into words.

"Why do I have to learn the alphabet or how to spell?" he complained to his par-

ents. "I want to be a baseball player, and they don't have to know the ABCs to hit a ball."

"Everyone needs to know the ABCs or they will get into trouble," Mother said. "But right now it's time to S-L-E-E-P. Good night!"

"'Night, M-O-M! 'Night, D-A-D!" Benji said as he turned over and closed his eyes.

BING! ! BING! Two strange characters were suddenly standing by Benji's bed.

"Who are you?" asked Benji.

"We are A to Z," Mr. A said. "And we have come to tell you how much you need us."

"What makes you think *I* need *you?*" Benji snapped.

"Well, you see," answered Mr. A, "without us you could have a lot of problems. But be-

fore I say more, I want you to meet my friends."

Soft music played while letters of every kind hopped down from nowhere and stood by Benji's bed.

"Wow," gasped Benji. "You sure have a lot of friends."

"That's right," said Mr. A. "And you need all of us to help you in your life."

Suddenly there was a loud GROWL!

"What's that?" asked Mrs. Z.

"It's just my stomach. I forgot to eat a bedtime snack and now I'm very hungry," Benji answered.

"That's too bad," replied Mr. A. "Would you like to have some C-A-T food?"

"Well, I guess so," said Benji, who had no idea what C-A-T food was.

Snap! Mr. A snapped his fingers and a big bowl of cat food appeared.

"Yuk! that's terrible!" yelled Benji.

"Oh," said Mr. A, "we're sorry, but you see we're not people and we don't know what kind of food you eat."

"Well, I don't eat cat food," Benji huffed.

"Then what would you like?" asked Mr. A.

"I want a hot dog," answered Benji. "And hurry, please. I'm very hungry."

"Can you spell it?" asked Mr. A.

"Spell it? Why do I have to spell it?" Benji asked.

Mr. A smiled and began to explain. "You see, Benji, in our land we cannot grant a request until you spell the thing you ask for. It may seem strange to you, but that's the law of Letter Land."

"Look," Benji complained, "I'm hungry and I want my hot dog NOW!"

"And you can have it," answered Mr. A. "If you know how to spell it."

"Maybe I can, and maybe I can't," Benji growled.

"But you must try," Mr. A replied.

"OK, then, let's see now," Benji said. "I think it begins with F. Yes, that's right. It's F-A-T. Now for the word *dog* . . . um . . . er, yes, I'm sure it's H-O-G."

Another snap of Mr. A's fingers and instantly a huge hog stood in front of Benji.

"A hog???" Benji cried. "But I didn't ask for a hog."

"Oh, but you did!" replied Mr. A. "That's what you spelled."

"Okay, that's it! Now, I'm *really* mad. I want to go home right now!" Benji shouted.

"Home?" asked Mrs. Z. "And how do you spell *home?*

"Oh, No!!!" groaned Benji. "I forgot that I have to spell out everything I need. I don't even know how to spell *home.*"

"Then. . .it looks like we have a BIG PROBLEM," said Mr. A. "Are you sure you can't spell *home?*"

"No!!! I really can't," cried Benji. "What am I going to do?"

"Maybe Mr. Bookworm can help us," suggested Mrs. Z. She gently knocked on the door of a house that looked like a dictionary. Soon a little worm opened the door.

"Good day, Mr. Bookworm," said Mrs. Z. "We are having a problem and I wonder if you can help us."

"Please, Mr. Bookworm," Benji said, "*I really am in trouble.* Can you help me?"

"As a matter of fact, I can," replied Mr. Bookworm. "But I won't!"

"You won't?" cried Benji. "Why?"

"Why should I? Spelling means nothing to you. You hate the alphabet, and you don't even want to learn," Mr. Bookworm snapped.

Tears began to fall down Benji's cheeks.

"I know," Benji said. "I really have been stubborn. But now I can see how important all of you and spelling are to me."

Mr. Bookworm looked at the alphabet letters. "Miss E, would you please come here? Oh, yes, and you too, Mrs. O and Mr. M. Now, Miss H, please stand here by me."

Each letter came quickly and stood by Mr. Bookworm.

"Suppose I did spell *home* for you." Mr. Bookworm said to Benji. "Then what

231

happens tomorrow? Will you forget everything that happened here?"

"Oh, no, Sir!" Benji promised. "I will
never forget what happened."

Mr. Bookworm could see that Benji
intended to keep his promise.

"Miss H, please stand here. Mrs. O,
stand between Miss H and Mr. M. Now,
Miss E, please stand on the other side of
Mr. M," said Mr. Bookworm.

All the letters lined up and Mr. Bookworm looked through his very thick
glasses at Benji. "Benji, do you promise to
remember what you have learned in Letter Land?"

"Yes, I promise," said Benji. "I will never forget and I promise always to do my homework—without grumbling."

Mr. Bookworm smiled and gave Benji a gentle hug.

"Okay, letters, let's spell H-O-M-E together, shall we?"

"Benji! Benji! It's time to wake up," Mother called.

"Wha. . .er. . .Ah. . .Mom, is that you? Well, what do you know? I'm home! HURRAY!!! HURRAY!!!"

"Did I hear you spell something?" Mother asked.

"You sure did, Mom. From now on I will be spelling ev-

ery day. I spent last night in Letter Land. While I was there I really learned a L-E-S-S-O-N," Benji said as he began to get ready for school.

A Friend for Fluffy

Four-year-old Terri got a very special birthday present—a little baby kitten. Terri named the kitten Fluffy because he had a fluff of fur around his neck.

Terri and Fluffy did everything together. When Terri was eating, Fluffy would sit under the table and play with Terri's shoestrings. At night, Fluffy would

climb up on Terri's bed and cuddle up on the pillow next to Terri.

Terri had to s c o l d Fluffy one day when she saw him trying to catch a gold-fish for lunch. Fluffy was sorry and promised never, never to try that again.

One morning, Fluffy was gone. He just disappeared. Terri looked in every corner of the house and in all of Fluffy's favorite hiding places, but Fluffy was NOT THERE.

All day Terri looked for Fluffy. She went up and down the street, calling his name. Fluffy didn't come home when it was time to eat. Fluffy didn't come home when it was time to go to bed. Terri was so sad. She cried and sobbed and then cried and sobbed some more.

Mother tucked Terri in at bedtime. When she was all alone in her room, Terri prayed, "Dear God, Oh, please don't let anything bad happen to Fluffy. He is only a little kitten and I am so sad and wor-ried about him. Will you please take good care of him? If he is lost, could you please let some little girl like me find him and

give him a good home? Thank you, God. Amen."

Terri had a dream that night. An angel came to talk to her.

"Terri, you must believe that everything will be OK. Don't worry about Fluffy, because God is taking care of him. God takes care of all of us. Just trust him."

Terri was so happy that she kissed the angel right on the nose.

The next morning Terri heard a tiny sound outside her window.

"I wonder if I am still dreaming," she

240

said. "That is such a small, soft sound."

She ran to the window, opened it, and looked down.

"Meow," said Fluffy happily.

Terri couldn't believe her eyes. THERE WAS FLUFFY!!! Her little kitten was getting a hug from a new friend, a brown-eyed puppy. They were tired and hungry because they had been in a big fight.

"So that's where you've been," Terri said. "I hope you have learned a lesson and will be good friends now. Come in, I'll feed both of you."

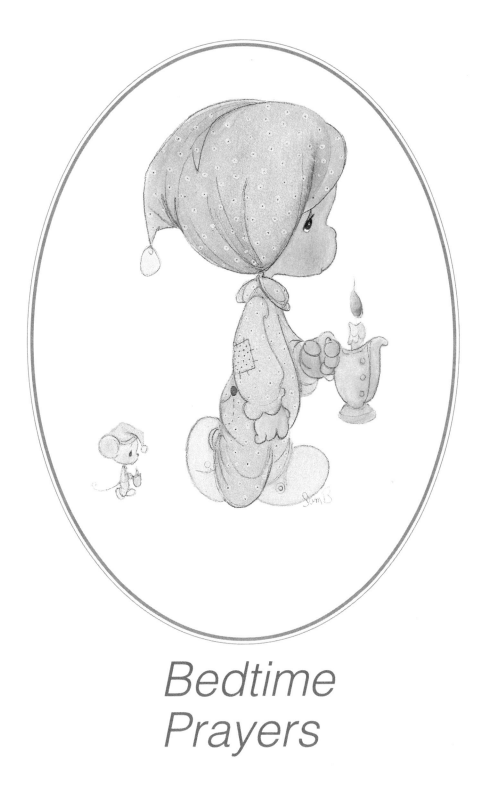

Bedtime
Prayers

Jesus, tender shepherd, hear
   me,
Bless thy little lamb tonight.
Through the darkness be thou
   near me,
Keep me safe till morning
   light.

Traditional

I thank you, loving Father,
For all your love today,
For sending Christ the
   Savior
To take my sins away.

Author Unknown

When I lie asleep at night,
Ever may your angels bright
Keep me safe till morning
 light:
Hear me, Holy Jesus

Thomas B. Pollock, 1971
Adapted

Father, I thank you for the night
And for the pleasant morning
    light,
For rest and food and loving care,
And all that makes the world so
    fair.

Help me to do the things I should,
To be to others kind and good,
In all I do in work or play
To be more loving every day.

Rebecca J. Weston, 1885
Adapted

My Own Bedtime Prayers

My Own Bedtime Prayers

My Own Bedtime Prayers

My Own Bedtime Prayers

My Own Bedtime Prayers

My Own Bedtime Prayers

My Own Bedtime Prayers